Frankenstein

Mary W. Shelley

ILLUSTRATED

Pendulum Press, Inc.

West Haven, Connecticut

ISBN 0-88301-093-3 Complete Set
       0-88301-097-6 This Volume

Library of Congress Catalog Card Number 73-75462

Published by
Pendulum Press, Inc.
An Academic Industries, Inc. Company
The Academic Building
Saw Mill Road
West Haven, Connecticut 06516

Printed in the United States of America

TO THE TEACHER

Pendulum Press is proud to offer the NOW AGE ILLUSTRATED Series to schools throughout the country. This completely new series has been prepared by the finest artists and illustrators from around the world. The script adaptations have been prepared by professional writers and revised by qualified reading consultants.

Implicit in the development of the Series are several assumptions. Within the limits of propriety, anything a child reads and/or wants to read is *per se* an educational tool. Educators have long recognized this and have clamored for materials that incorporate this premise. The sustained popularity of the illustrated format, for example, has been documented, but it has not been fully utilized for educational purposes. Out of this realization, the NOW AGE ILLUSTRATED Series evolved.

In the actual reading process, the illustrated panel encourages and supports the student's desire to read printed words. The combination of words and picture helps the student to a greater understanding of the subject; and understanding, that comes from reading, creates the desire for more reading.

The final assumption is that reading as an end in itself is self-defeating. Children are motivated to read material that satisfies their quest for knowledge and understanding of their world. In this series, they are exposed to some of the greatest stories, authors, and characters in the English language. The Series will stimulate their desire to read the original edition when their reading skills are sufficiently developed. More importantly, reading books in the NOW AGE ILLUSTRATED Series will help students establish a mental "pegboard" of information — images, names, and concepts — to which they are exposed. Let's assume, for example, that a child sees a television commercial which features Huck Finn in some way. If he has read the NOW AGE Huck Finn, the TV reference has meaning for him which gives the child a surge of satisfaction and accomplishment.

After using the NOW AGE ILLUSTRATED editions, we know that you will share our enthusiasm about the series and its concept.

—The Editors

ABOUT THE AUTHOR

Mary Shelley was born in 1797, the daughter of a well-known political philosopher and an ardent feminist. Her mother died shortly after her birth, her father remarried and Mary was subjected to an abusing stepmother. Her life was unhappy until she met Percy Bysshe Shelley whom she eventually married.

It was during an evening with Lord Byron in Switzerland that the plot for *Frankenstein* was first conceived. *Frankenstein* is concerned with the principle of life, and with man's overweening ability to tamper with it. Dr. Frankenstein oversteps the normal human bounds and creates a monster.

The monster at first is basically good, but through loneliness and rejection, he turns evil. He is forced to prey on man to survive. The resulting tale is gripping and memorable.

Mary Shelley

FRANKENSTEIN

Adapted by
OTTO BINDER

Illustrated by
NARDO CRUZ

a
VINCENT FAGO
production

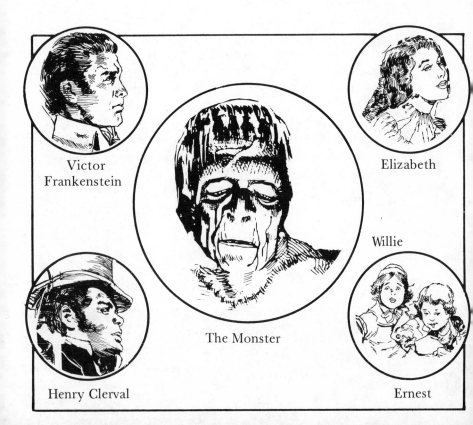

Victor
Frankenstein

Elizabeth

Willie

The Monster

Henry Clerval

Ernest

Frankenstein wanted fame as a scientist. He wanted to find the secrets of life so that all people could live without the fear of death. But something went wrong—his creation was a monster, ugly and strong. Even Frankenstein could not look on his creation with love—but only with fear. No one gave the monster a chance. All he looked for was friendship until he found that no one would love him. Then he wanted revenge. . . .

There lived a happy family in Geneva, Switzerland, in the mid-1700s.

FATHER

VICTOR

MOTHER

ERNEST

ELIZABETH

WILLIAM

After posing for this portrait painted by an artist. . .

It was nice of you to have me in the picture since I'm not really one of the Frankenstein family!

What does it matter that your parents are dead, my dear, whom we took into our family? We love you just as we do our own three boys, even though we say to others you are their "cousin."

And I love you like brothers.

Me, too, Elizabeth?

Of course, Ernest!

And me, dear Elizabeth? Do you love me like a brother?

Oh, Victor! You are making me blush!

You know I love you in a very special way!

Those are the words I hoped to hear, my sweet "cousin!"

Then one terrible day, Madame Frankenstein became ill and died.

My children, my hopes of future happiness came from knowing that you two would marry. I still hope the marriage will take place after I'm gone.

After his mother died, young Victor Franken-stein's thoughts were filled with the idea that he would soon go to college.

I already know a lot about science. I want to learn more of the secrets about nature.

I know about the laws of electricity. I shall study all the natural sciences.

But most of all, I want to carefully study chemistry and how it affects the biology of life. How famous I'd be, if I could do away with human sickness and make men safe except for death by accident.

Finally the day he was to leave came.

Goodbye, father! Be good, Ernest and Willie!

We'll all miss you, my boy!

I'm going to miss you most of all, Victor!

Dear Elizabeth! May time go by quickly while I'm gone. When I return from the university. . .well, we shall see!

Also there with good wishes was Victor's boyhood friend, Henry Clerval.

I wish I could get an education, too, Victor. But my father says I must work in his business.

Too bad, Henry! Come and see me when you can. Good-bye!

Somewhat sadly, young Victor Frankenstein darted into the carriage for his journey away from home.

I know I'll be sad and lonely, leaving my family and friends! But I look forward to studying science, my great interest, at the university!

And so it was that young Victor Frankenstein, filled with high hopes, went to college in Ingolstadt, in the high Alps.

I'll study chemistry and find a new way to look into unknown powers, and show the world the deepest mysteries of creation!

M. Krempe, Frankenstein's first teacher, was a strange man but he knew much about the secrets of science.

How can I hope to learn all I must know!

You must read, my boy. Read everything you can find and study what is said.

The young student learned much from his hours with M. Waldman, the famous natural scientist.

My eyes are opening to new things from your classes, sir.

Good, my boy! Scientists are making great discoveries. They have discovered how the blood circulates, and the nature of the air we breathe, and many new things.

But I want to find out more. What causes life?

What causes the human body to wear out and die?

Can I possibly find the way to bring life to unliving matter?

Frankenstein began to work on creating life. He searched in graveyards and morgues* for dead bodies on which he could experiment.

Lifeless bodies! If I can create life from this, it will be a new kind of man. And I will make him smarter then other men!

*places where bodies are stored until they are buried.

For his horrible experiments, Frankenstein found an old house, set off by itself.

I cannot tell Professor Waldman, or my other teachers, what I am working on. They might consider it against God!

The rest of the time he was an excellent student, and two years later, Frankenstein earned the praise of his teacher.

Only your mind, my dear Frankenstein, could have made these discoveries.

Thank you, sir.

Not at all, my boy! In fact, you have left us all behind in your studies. You've set yourself at the head of the college in chemistry! You, just a youngster! You can be proud!

But Frankenstein had greater desires and worked nightly at his secret experiment.

Am I getting closer to my goal? Will this new chemical bring life to a man made up of the dead flesh I've put together?

And on a dark night in November, a strange event took place.

Can I give life to this lifeless creature, put together by my own hands? Will my chemical work and give him life?

If so, a new kind of life will bless me as its creator! I made him very large, eight feet tall. Ah! He moved an arm!

Now let me see the result of my work.

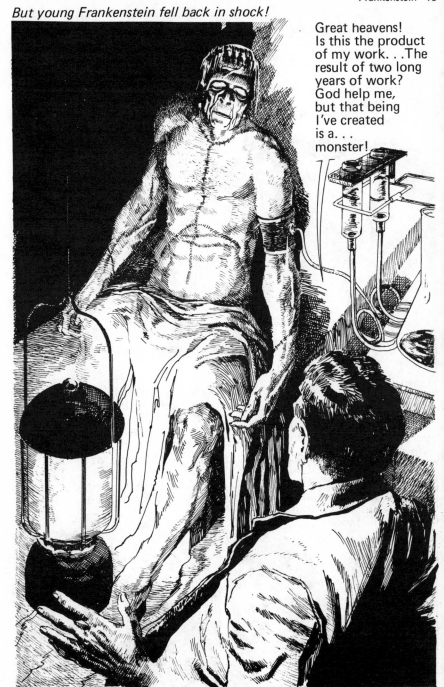

Unable to stand looking at the being he had created, Frankenstein rushed out of the room.

At first, in his bedroom, he could not get to sleep, but at last. . . .

The beauty of my dream has disappeared, and I am afraid of what I've done!

I'm tired. . . I must rest.

During the night he awoke frightened and saw what the yellow light of the moon showed him.

Frankenstein rushed downstairs to the courtyard and walked up and down for the rest of the night.

It's that creature. . .the miserable monster I created! He's staring at me. . .making strange sounds. . .with a smile on his face.

Ulgg? Ulgg?

I fear each sound, as if it were to tell of the coming of that horrible body to which I gave life.

The next day, Frankenstein was surprised when a visitor arrived in Ingolstadt.

Henry! Henry Clerval, my old friend!

Greetings, my dear Frankenstein! But how ill you look, so thin and pale. What is wrong?

At his house, Frankenstein had Clerval stay outside a few moments while he checked the house.

I'm afraid to look at the monster, but I fear still more that Henry should see him! I must see where the creature is hiding.

After looking in all the rooms. . . .

All empty! I can hardly believe my good luck. My enemy has gone. I could clap my hands for joy.

But later, as they had breakfast together, Frankenstein saw a terrible sight before his eyes.

Is that ghost coming into the room? Save me. . .save me. . . ohhhhh!

Frankenstein! He's fainting, poor chap. He must be very ill.

Frankenstein was very ill. It was the beginning of a fever that kept him in bed for several months, with his friend Clerval as his nurse.

He's dreaming again!

The monster!. . .that devil to whom I gave life! He is always in front of my eyes!

Meanwhile, after escaping from Frankenstein's house, the poor monster ran into the woods near Ingolstadt.

Before long he was hungry and thirsty and found that berries could fill him.

After a night's sleep in the forest, the creature felt cold and happened to find a large cape lost by someone.

As he wandered about, he began to watch the living things that were around him, especially birds, whose songs he tried to copy.

As the days passed, the homeless creature learned which kind of berries and plants he could eat.

Knowing less than a child, the monster one day learned a painful lesson when he came upon a fire left by someone.

But then, liking the warmth of the fire, he thought about it and finally found out what would keep it from dying out.

He slept that night near the warm fire, then left to hunt more food to feed his large body. He found that nuts and roots were good.

Reaching the edge of the forest, the monster first met up with snow and bitter cold.

Seeing a hut whose door was open, the monster walked in, scaring an old man who sat by the fire.

The creature was upset at the way the old man acted but he found food and ate the bread, cheese, milk, and wine, which were all new to him.

God save me! What is that horrible ghost? Help!

When he came to a village the next day, the poor monster was even more upset at the actions of the people.

How horrible! Run, children!

Help!

Help!

He ran across the fields to get away from the angry crowd. The poor creature found a hut that looked empty and hid there.

Something told the creature to make his hiding place safe, by closing up cracks inside the broken down shack with boards.

After an uneasy, but safe sleep, the creature saw that his shack was attached to a cottage. Cooling on the windowsill of the cottage he also found bread.

Later that day, the monster saw the people who lived in the cottage returning from their work.

The monster then found a crack in the wall that let him look right into the cottage.

Three people lived in the cottage, the couple and an old man. The old man began to play a musical instrument, and the monster was pleased by music sweeter than the voice of any bird.

He watched closely every day, and found that the old man was blind, and also that the people were very poor and ate small meals.

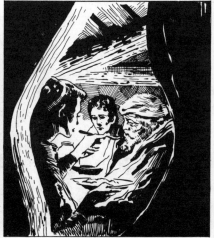

In his human-like mind, the monster felt he should help his friends in some way, and during the night, using the young farmer's cutting tools, he cut wood for their fire.

In the morning, the people were very surprised when they saw the large pile of firewood outside,

Slowly, the monster made a discovery of even greater value. He found the people had a way of understanding one another—by means of spoken words.

Heavens! It's the work of a good spirit!

It saves me a lot of work.

Br-bread? Milk? Wood?

As the weeks passed, he listened carefully, and learned other words with deeper meanings, and also heard names.

Agatha, my dearest sister! You never complain about how poor we are!

It does not make me unhappy, Felix.

Good. . .dearest. . . poor. . .unhappy! Ag-agatha?. . .Felix?

He made another discovery! Felix read from a book to his sister and the old man, as if there were signs on the paper for the very words the monster had learned by ear.

. . . .good. . .dearest. . . unhappy. . . .

One day, the monster happened to look down into a puddle left by rain, and was filled with sadness at first sight of his ugliness, so unlike the way the people in the cottage looked.

When winter ended and spring came, the monster who ate only vegetables ate well from a garden grown by the cottage people.

And again, the monster returned the favor by doing a job he had watched Felix do during the day, pulling weeds.

Something new happened in summer. A visitor came, a lady who seemed to bring joy to Felix's heart.

Safie, my darling! I'm so happy that you finally left your foreign land and came here, but of course you do not understand our language, I will teach you!

Whatever the stranger learned from Felix, the listening monster also learned! So he quickly learned the language.

Mystery. . .something unknown. Conversation . . .talking. Peaceful. . . not war-like.

I understand, Felix. I am learning quickly.

One day, the monster learned that Safie was from Arabia.* He was sad because he belonged to no one and no place.

What. . .am. . .I? I. . .have. . . no mother or father! No relatives! I was. . .created just as I am. . .of full size! I was never a baby! I don't belong to any humans!

* a penninsula in Southwestern Asia

Sneaking into the cottage at night, the creature who wanted to learn, looked over the books Felix had read, and fit words he had heard to the printed words.

Ah, g-o-o-d must be good! When I have matched all the spoken and written words I learned from Felix, I will be able to read books and learn more.

He found he could read almost everything.

These books make me feel and think about all kinds of things. Sometimes they make me happy and sometimes sad.

As he learned more about the world and life, through the books, he began to ask more questions about himself.

What am I? My face is ugly and I am too tall. What will happen to me? Will people always hate me and stay away from me because I'm so ugly?

Then one day, looking through the pockets of the clothes he had taken from Victor Frankenstein's laboratory, the monster found notes Frankenstein had written.

Every step he followed in creating me is here. Everything he did is written down.

...I Frankenstein, am an accursed creator for forming a monster so hideous!

Even my creator turned from me in fear!

I even hate myself!
Oh, the terrible day that I was created in a laboratory!

The creature grew more and more unhappy.

Adam, created by God, had his Eve. But where is my Eve? I have been left alone by everyone.

I am the ugliest creature on earth, in all history!

One day, Frankenstein's monster looked through his crack into the cottage.

The others have left for a walk, leaving the old man DeLacey alone! He's playing his guitar. Since he is blind, he will not see my horrible body if I enter and speak to him!

The monster knocked on the door and was told to come in. He had his story ready.

Oh, if I could only make him my friend!

I am a traveller who needs to rest. Will you let me stay a few minutes before the fire!

Sit down, please.

Hopefully, the monster told his story.

But at that moment, the very people he spoke of came in, showing fear and surprise at the huge, ugly visitor.

I am a poor and unhappy creature. I am an enemy of the world forever unless certain friendly people take me for what I am.

He does not know I'm speaking of Felix, Agatha, and Safie!

What is that fearful creature? Ohhhh!

Save and protect me, DeLacey! You and your family are the friends I meant!

Leave my poor father alone, you devil! Get out!

Why doesn't he see I mean no harm? Does the way I look make everyone hate me?

Filled with unhappiness, the creature ran to his hiding place.

Must it always be this way? Must the humans always think I am going to hurt them? Can they not see that I long for friendship?

When night came, the poor creature ran into the forest and let out his feelings in loud cries.

Something seemed to snap within him and terrible words came from his lips.

I see now that no one will feel sorry or help me. From this moment on, I declare war against all human beings!

And especially against the one who made me and sent me to this terrible life, Victor Frankenstein!

So frightened were Felix and his family that the next day they moved from the cottage, never to return.

We would never recover if we saw that monster again! We must find a new home.

They have left me. My heart only has room for the hate of men.

Later, not able to find humans to hurt, the monster took out his hate on non-living things.

I destroyed every bit of the garden! Now to burn the cottage!

That night, overcome by a kind of madness, the creature set fire to the cottage and flames began to jump around it.

Burn! Burn! I will wreck all human things for their owners are my enemies! I will destroy. . .smash. . . kill. . .up and down the world! Yaaaaaaaaaa!

The monster danced around the burning cottage, yelling about the things he would do to people who would not be his friend, and treated him cruelly.

By morning, when the cottage was nothing but ashes, he became a cold, angry fighter, planning his first acts against his enemy.

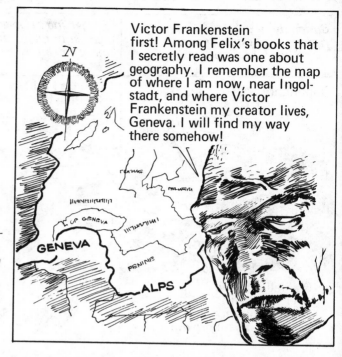

Victor Frankenstein first! Among Felix's books that I secretly read was one about geography. I remember the map of where I am now, near Ingolstadt, and where Victor Frankenstein my creator lives, Geneva. I will find my way there somehow!

Through the autumn. . .and winter. . .and then spring, the monster walked, staying away from humans, not asking directions and often losing the way, but always getting closer to his goal.

Suddenly, a young girl came running alongside a river, when her feet slipped.

Forgetting his anger against humans, the monster ran from hiding.

Ohhhhhhh!

She fell into the river. The swift current will carry her away. She'll drown!

Caught her! Now I'll drag her to shore.

But when the man she was with came up. . . .

Are you a devil from the world of the dead? Let her alone!

He shot me! I was only trying to save her, and this is what I get for trying.

The monster escaped but in the weeks that followed he had terrible pain from the wound and even greater pain in his thoughts.

His wound healed by the time he reached the city of Geneva.

The young man didn't understand that I didn't want to hurt her. My only thought was to save the girl's life.

I'll rest here first and then find Victor Frankenstein's home and punish him!

But a child came through the forest, and the monster had a new idea.

If I can teach this little boy to be my friend, I will not be so lonely.

Stop screaming, boy. I will not hurt you. Just listen to me.

No! Let me go! You are a monster and you wish to tear me to pieces and eat me! Let me go or my father will punish you! His name is. . . .

. . . .M. Frankenstein!

Frankenstein? Then this boy is Victor Frankenstein's brother! And he shall be my first victim!

The monster's hand closed around the child's throat, tighter and tighter, until. . . .

Dead! The death of his young brother will bring pain to Victor Frankenstein. . .the first of more to come!

The monster found a small picture around the boy's neck.

Lovely! But I am forever without the love of such beautiful creatures! However, if she is loved by Victor Frankenstein, I will not let him have her either.

Leaving the murder spot, the monster looked for a hiding place and entered a barn, to make another discovery.

A young woman sleeping here! If she awakens and sees me, she will later tell the police and they will know I am the murderer of the boy!

I will hide this picture I took from the boy in her pocket! And everyone will think she murdered the boy.

After the boy's body was discovered, the police found the girl, Justine Moritz, in the barn.

Look! The very picture that they said the boy carried with him! You murdered him!

No, no! Why I loved little William Frankenstein! This is some terrible mistake!

But no one believed her, and the unlucky girl was found guilty.

You have been proven guilty of the crime of murder! The court sentences you, Justine Moritz, to be killed!

Nobody thinks I did it! That girl dies, like the boy! My second blow against my human enemies!

Saddened terribly by the death of his younger brother, Victor Frankenstein one day climbed a mountain to seek peace for his heart, when suddenly. . . .

What's that running and jumping at superhuman speed? Great God! It's my monster!

You are here? You, with all your evil ugliness? Go away.

Not before I tell you something that will crush your soul.

It was I, not your good friend, who killed your little brother William!

You did, you devil? Then I must put out the spark of life which I so carelessly gave you!

You can't hurt me. You gave me more-than-human strength, if you'll remember, my dear creator!

Hold, and listen! I will kill all your friends and dear ones, unless you grant me one wish.

What is your wish, then?

Frankenstein's blood ran cold as he heard the terrible answer!

You must create a female for me!

What? Shall I create another like you so that together you might destroy the world?

But the monster begged Frankenstein to listen.

My loneliness makes me do terrible things.

You must create a creature of the other sex for me! We will be monsters cut off from the world, and we will harm no one.

If you do as I ask, I promise that no human being will see us again. We will go to the wilds of South America to live.

Frankenstein listened and after much thought, made up his mind.

I will grant your wish, if you will leave Europe forever!

If you grant my prayer, you shall never see me again!

The monster left suddenly.

He is going down the mountain faster than an eagle can fly!

When Victor Frankenstein went back to his family, he felt he had done right in promising to make a female for the monster.

My father. . .dear Elizabeth. . .my brother Ernest! To save them from the monster's anger, I promise to do that dreadful thing. I have no choice.

Before he could begin his work. . . .

I cannot make the female monster without again spending weeks or months in careful study.

But Frankenstein's father was upset that the marriage was put off.

The dearest wish of your mother before she died, and also I, was to see the marriage of your "cousin" and you. Have you changed your mind?

No, father! I love Elizabeth dearly. But I have an important job I must do first.

Before the marriage of Elizabeth and myself, the monster must get his bride. . .and leave!

I must find some quiet place in northern Scotland to finish my work. My good friend Henry Clerval will be the only one who will know where I am.

Frankenstein finally picked one of the far away gray Orkney Islands.

It is little more than a rock, the perfect place for being quiet and alone.

There are only three huts on the whole island, and I rented this one. Terrible place but it is well suited to my terrible work.

Frankenstein then began working day and night.

It is a horrible thing that I am doing, and I find it hard at times to go on. My heart often gets sick. But I dare not stop.

Three years ago I was doing this same thing, when I created a monster, who is the ugliest thing in the world. Now I must make another such terrible creature.

Frankenstein wondered sometimes if a female would be all the monster wanted.

Oh God—what if he comes back and asks for children. I could be cursing the world forever.

One day, the monster himself came to watch.

I followed you all the way here, Frankenstein, to make certain you were keeping your promise.

Oh! That horrible face! Those evil eyes! Now I am sorry for my promise!

Suddenly, Frankenstein destroyed the thing he had half-made!

No! I will not do this terrible thing! There! It is destroyed!

When he saw Frankenstein destroy the creature he was waiting for, the monster gave a cry and ran away.

My bride-to-be! My friend in an unfriendly world. . . gone! All my dreams gone!

Later, while Frankenstein hurriedly packed. . . .

I hear the door opening! Is it the monster coming back?

Are you going to break your promise to me, keeping from me a friend who would take away my loneliness?

I do break my promise, devil! Never will I create another like yourself!

Fool! Before I begged you, but now I see I will have to show you I mean business. You are my creator, but now I am your master! Obey me and finish your task!

Shall I put two devils on the earth who will kill humans? Go away! You cannot frighten me!

I go. But remember — I shall be with you on your wedding night!

He is leaving the island. I gave that monster such strength that his boat shoots across the waters with an arrow's swiftness!

Those words made Frankenstein's blood cold in his veins.

Frankenstein was left alone hearing fearful words in his mind.

Moving himself at last, Frankenstein gathered up the thing he had destroyed, and later. . . .

I cannot leave anything of my work to frighten and worry the people of the island. The basket is filled with stones and will sink to the bottom of the sea!

I will leave immediately, and sail to the mainland.

But a storm came up, and his sailboat was driven far out at sea, in danger of being sunk.

But chance brought him to a strange shore, where. . . .

Would you good people tell me where I am?

Ireland, sir! And you must follow me to tell who you are. You see, a gentleman was found murdered here last night!

The body was found strangled, and was washed in by the sea. . .from the very direction you came from. We will see if you know him and will confess when you see your evil deed.

I am not worried for I killed no one.

But when Frankenstein saw the dead man's face, a great shock ran through him!

Henry? Henry Clerval! Has the monster killed you also? For you were strangled just as little Willie was. . .by the same hand!

He was so shocked that he was very sick for two months. He recovered one day to find. . . .

I thought I was dead!

Better for you if you were dead, sir. For you are said to have killed that man. They have been waiting to bring you to trial.

But Frankenstein was easily found not guilty by the jury.

Facts clearly show that this man, Victor Frankenstein, was in Orkney Islands on the date of the murder. Release him!

Victor's father took him on a trip to Paris, to help him get over his illness.

Father! Listen to me! I am the cause of the deaths of little Willie, of poor Justine, and my friend Henry Clerval. They all died by my hands.

You are mad, son, or kidding!

Victor could not make himself tell of his created creature.

I am not mad. And it is no joke. I tell you I am the killer of those three innocent victims!

His mind is upset from his long illness. He will get better in time and forget his wrong ideas!

But Victor had still more shocking words for his father.

Because of my terrible deeds, I cannot marry Elizabeth, though I love her deeply!

Victor!

The true reason that I cannot wed my beloved is because of those frightful words the monster spoke.

I shall be with you on your wedding night!

When Victor Frankenstein returned home and met Elizabeth, they set the wedding date.

And guess what, darling? I have just inherited some property in Austria. We will spend our honeymoon at Lake Como in the Villa Lavenza.

But after the older Frankenstein had written Elizabeth telling all that had been said, a letter from her changed Victor's mind.

...*I love you. You need explain nothing. And all my future happiness resides in living with you as your loving wife.*

I cannot destroy all her dreams of happiness! I will marry her and see what the monster does!

But still worried by the monster's promise, Frankenstein tried to protect Elizabeth and himself from the monster.

I'll carry guns. The monster will not be able to hurt us.

And so, the wedding took place at Geneva.

As planned, the bride and groom left on a lake steamer to Elizabeth's property on the shores of Como.

It was still daylight and when they parted for a moment. . . .

I want to freshen up, dear!

And I'm going to check every corner of this house where the monster might hide.

He searched carefully and just as he began to feel safe. . . .

I've searched everywhere but no sign of the monster, thank heavens. Wait! That scream! Is it Elizabeth?

Did the monster stay hidden all the while in Elizabeth's room. The one room I didn't search? I hope my fears are wrong.

But they weren't.

Then, with a feeling of horror, Frankenstein saw the monster at the open window, laughing and pointing at the dead woman.

"You must die, you devil!"

"You'll never hit me, fool!"

People came running from nearby at the sound of the gunshot and boats were put out with nets, but. . . .

"We caught nothing, sir! The murderer has disappeared.

He is so fast and so strong."

Frankenstein remembered the terrible things that had happened to his loved ones.

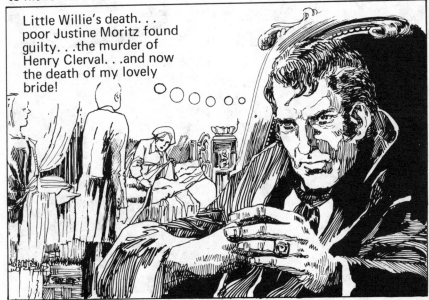

"Little Willie's death. . . poor Justine Moritz found guilty. . .the murder of Henry Clerval. . .and now the death of my lovely bride!"

And soon after, another victim was added to the list when Victor Frankenstein returned to his home.

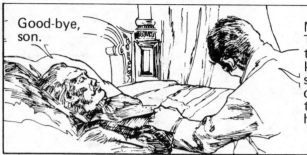

Good-bye, son.

My father, dead! Though not right there, the monster killed him as surely as if his cruel hands had tightened around his throat!

Feeling sick and weak, young Frankenstein suffered another illness this time so bad that. . . .

Months later when he was better, Frankenstein visited a cemetery which held his family's graves, to make a promise.

Poor soul, he went quite mad! It will be months before he can be let go! He groans and moans from morning till night!

I swear by all that is holy to find the devil who killed you!

Upon leaving the grave. . . .

That laughter. . . who is it?

Ha! Haaa! Are you unhappy now, like I am?

I shall track him somehow, even to the very ends of the earth!

Frankenstein chased the monster and picked up his trail at the Mediterranean. . . .

I saw the devil board a ship for the Black Sea, but too late to stop him. I'll take this next ship to the same place.

The hunt continued into Russia, where people gave Frankenstein information about his monster.

As near as I can make it, from his signs, a large man passed this way yesterday, heading north. . .far north!

Frankenstein thought he had lost his trail when one day. . . .

The monster's footprint! Is he leaving signs for me to follow on purpose, leading me on and on?

It was so. Signs were left behind by the monster, leading Frankenstein on into the northern wilderness.

The monster left a mark out in the bark of this tree, showing me which way he went.

MY REIGN IS NOT YET OVER! FOLLOW ME TO THE EVERLASTING ICE OF THE NORTHLAND

EAT AND PRESERVE YOUR STRENGHT! YOU WILL SOON FEEL THE MISERY OF INTENSE COLD TO WHICH I AM IMPASSIVE!!

I will freeze to death unless I wear fur clothing of Arctic explorers!

I rented a sled and dog team! The monster's last message said that we must meet in the north, at a spot, and fight for our lives!

He has a dog sled, too, and the tracks lead away from the land, out over the frozen sea itself! I will not give up until I run him down!

The monster, just a mile ahead! Faster, dogs, faster!

But spring was coming to the North and a loud crack ended the race.

The spring thaw! The ice is cracking into pieces!

Frankenstein was left floating on a huge piece of ice.

A piece of the ice broke free. This must be the end for me.

But before Frankenstein died, a ship appeared, and. . . .

And aboard the ship, Frankenstein lay ill and very thin, slowly getting worse as the days passed.

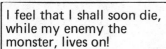

And finally, Frankenstein died.

But that night, when the captain heard a sound in the dead man's room. . . .

Great God! The very monster Frankenstein talked about. Then you are real and you are the evil creature who took so many lives!

Yes, and Victor Frankenstein is also my victim at last!

But then, the monster showed his guilt and sorrow. . . .

Oh, Frankenstein. You were a good man. What good does it do me to tell you I'm sorry? You are dead and cannot hear me.

Why, the monster has a change of heart and is filled with sorrow at his awful crimes.

Do not think badly of me Captain! All I wanted was love and friendship from human beings, but people ran from me. If I have sinned, then all humans have sinned against me!

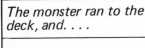

The monster ran to the deck, and. . . .

Fear not, I shall not hurt anyone else. My creator was my last victim. Farewell!

The monster is not really guilty of those murders. Men forced him to murder by their own cruelty to him. This monster is the victim of Frankenstein's wish to create a new kind of life. Let men remember that he failed.

WORDS TO KNOW

chemical   create   revenge
circulates   creature
communicating   monster

QUESTIONS

1. Why did young Frankenstein want to create new life?

2. How does the monster learn to speak and read?

3. What is the only thing the monster really wants out of life?

4. List some of the happenings from the story which show that the monster was not all bad.

5. What strange request does the monster make of Frankenstein?

6. Why doesn't Frankenstein keep his promise to the monster?

7. What does the word *revenge* mean? Who wants revenge in the story?

8. At the end of the story, why does the ship's captain pity the monster?